DISNEY

THE ILLUSTRATED

TREASURY OF SONGS

PIANO • VOCAL • GUITAR

HYPERION

NEW YORK

Hal Leonard Publishing Corporation

7777 West Bluemound Road P.O. Box 13819 Milwaukee, WI 53213

Copublished in 1993 by Hal Leonard Publishing Corporation,
Milwaukee, Wisconsin and Hyperion, New York

No part of this book may be used or reproduced in any
manner whatsoever without written permission of the Publisher

ISBN: 1-56282-743-X

FIRST EDITION
10 9 8 7 6 5 4 3 2 1

Printed in China

CONTENTS

INTRODUCTION

Walt Disney didn't read or write music. In fact, he never even played an instrument, unless you count an unsuccessful stab at the violin during grade school in Kansas City.

And yet his influence upon music was, and continues to be, so profound that the great American composer Jerome Kern was moved to say, "Disney has made use of music as language. In the synchronization of humorous episodes with humorous music, he has unquestionably given us the outstanding contribution of our time."

That's lofty praise, especially coming as it did from a musical legend like Kern. But what makes his words all the more amazing is the fact that he said them in 1936, *before* the release of *Snow White and the Seven Dwarfs*, arguably one of Walt Disney's greatest moments not only in animation, but music as well.

Still, the question remains: if Walt didn't write any songs or compose any scores, how could he have had such a deep and lasting impact on music?

The answer, simply enough, is the same way in which he had such a profound effect upon animation without so much as drawing even one mouse or dwarf.

Walt was the mover and shaker, the man of vision who gathered around him some of the most talented writers, artists, composers and musicians, who bought into his dreams and schemes and made them happen, all under his watchful eye.

"There's a terrific power to music. You can run any of these pictures and they'd be dragging and boring, but the minute you put music behind them, they have life and vitality they don't get any other way."

—Walt Disney

Walt and Roy Disney with the special "Oscar" awarded to Walt in 1932 for the creation of Mickey Mouse.

Disney's imprimatur is stamped onto every song . . .

He once described his role this way:

My role? Well, you know I was stumped one day when a little boy asked, "Do you draw Mickey Mouse?" I had to admit I do not draw anymore. "Then you think up the jokes and ideas?" "No," I said, "I don't do that." Finally, he looked at me and said, "Mr. Disney, just what do you do?" "Well," I said, "sometimes I think of myself as a little bee. I go from one area of the Studio to another and gather pollen and sort of stimulate everybody. I guess that's the job I do."

Of course, that doesn't explain Walt Disney's uncanny feel for what worked and what didn't, be it in music, films or theme parks. Perhaps Eric Sevareid summed it up best in his tribute to Walt on the *CBS Evening News* the day Disney died: "He was an original; not just an American original, but an original, period. He was a happy accident; one of the happiest this century has experienced . . . . People are saying we'll never see his like again."

Maybe it was his Midwestern upbringing and mid-American, mainstream appreciation for music and movies, or maybe he *was* just "a happy accident," but Walt Disney aimed to create entertainment that he himself would enjoy. Could he help it if hundreds of millions of people around the world happened to agree with him?

So although he didn't write "When You Wish Upon a Star," "Zip-A-Dee-Doo-Dah" or any of the other hundreds of tunes that make up the Disney canon, his imprimatur is stamped onto every song and score. When you hear "Whistle While You Work," you may not know that the words were written by Larry Morey and the music by Frank Churchill, but you certainly know it's a Disney song.

It didn't matter what a composer's background was, whether he was a honky-tonk pianist from Los Angeles, a jingle writer from New York's Tin Pan Alley or a pop star from England, when he wrote for Walt Disney he wrote in a style that was, consciously or not, immediately recognizable not as his own, but as Walt Disney's.

"No matter what I or anyone else in the music department wrote, people always recognized it as being the 'Disney sound,'" says Buddy Baker, a longtime Disney staff composer. "But if I was asked to define the Disney sound or how we got it, I would have to answer that I didn't know. It's not something I thought about while I was writing the music.

"I think a clue to the Disney sound, though, comes from the man himself," he adds. "Walt Disney had a wonderful concept of what the music should be, which is a great clue for the composer. For instance, if he wanted a big, symphonic score, he'd tell you that and he'd even tell you what he'd want it to sound like."

Disney songs represent a style and sprightliness that make them eminently hummable and totally unforgettable. They were very much a reflection of their patron, who concentrated on melody and didn't like anything that was too loud or high-pitched.

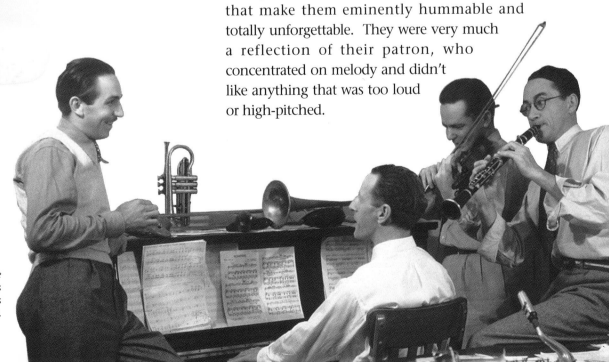

Music lightens a story session in the mid-1930s as Walt Disney visits (from left) Webb Smith, Ted Sears and Pinto Colvig.

Even the "Disney" songs and scores being written today, a whole quarter of a century after Walt Disney's death, reflect the spirit and influence of this man who had a special ability to recognize what kind of music best fit a scene or situation and, more importantly (and more to the point), what was good.

It was Walt's direction and influence that led his composers and musicians to pioneer musical concepts and technologies that influenced both the film and music industries for decades – and continue to do so to this day.

But the music didn't start out as Disney's own. In the first several Mickey Mouse cartoons, produced in 1928 and 1929, the music was either borrowed or adapted. An example was Mickey's very first cartoon, *Steamboat Willie*, released in November, 1928, and featuring the songs "Steamboat Bill" and "Turkey in the Straw."

(Top) Walt Disney's classic portrait with Mickey Mouse, taken at the Disney Studios on Hyperion Avenue in the 1930's. (Right) In 1938, Disney purchased undeveloped property in Burbank, which soon became the permanent home to the new Walt Disney Studios.

Walt created entertainment that he himself would enjoy

Still, even if the music wasn't written by members of Walt's staff, it was arranged in such a way that it sounded as if it just might have been. For instance, "Steamboat Bill," written in 1910, was whistled by the mouse himself during the opening moments of the cartoon.

THE EARLY YEARS

The sound that played the key role in Disney cartoons was music.

"Turkey in the Straw," which dates as far back as 1834 and is arguably a sing-song classic in the tradition of "Camptown Races" and "My Darling Clementine," was not arranged for normal instruments, such as guitars, flutes or pianos, but was instead configured to accommodate the variety of "instruments" Mickey plays during the cartoon, including a washboard, pots and pans, a cat, a duck, several suckling pigs and a cow's teeth. ("Turkey in the Straw," by the way, was selected for *Steamboat Willie* because it was one of the only tunes a young assistant animator named Wilfred Jackson, the sole musician at the small Disney Studios, could play on the harmonica.)

It could be said that the Disney musical legacy actually did begin with Walt himself. In 1929, he teamed with his then-musical director Carl Stalling to write a song that would become an anthem of sorts for his already famous star, Mickey Mouse.

That song, "Minnie's Yoo Hoo," was first heard in the 1929 short "Mickey's Follies." It is the only song for which Walt Disney ever took a writing credit.

Mickey Mouse and the musical improvisation that made him famous in his debut film, Steamboat Willie.

But that doesn't mean Walt didn't play an active role in the creation of the music heard in all succeeding Disney Studio cartoon shorts and animated features. He simply entrusted it to more accomplished composers and arrangers, the first of which was Stalling, an old friend from Kansas City.

Mickey Mouse shorts. Walt wanted Stalling to fit the music to the action, while Stalling felt the action should fit the music.

The Silly Symphonies were a compromise. In the Mickey cartoons, the music would continue to play second fiddle to the characters and the action, but in the Silly Symphonies the music would rule.

Stalling stayed with the Studio less than two years, jumping from Silly Symphonies at Disney to Looney Tunes and Merrie Melodies at Warner Brothers, where he created his own musical legacy composing scores for the likes of Bugs Bunny, Daffy Duck and Porky Pig.

Despite Stalling's departure, the Silly Symphonies continued. In fact, they became so popular that Walt Disney began beefing up his music staff in the early '30s to handle the increased need for music for them.

In "Silly Symphonies" the music would rule

It was Stalling who persuaded Walt to begin the Silly Symphony cartoon series, which grew out of disagreements the two had over the use of music in the

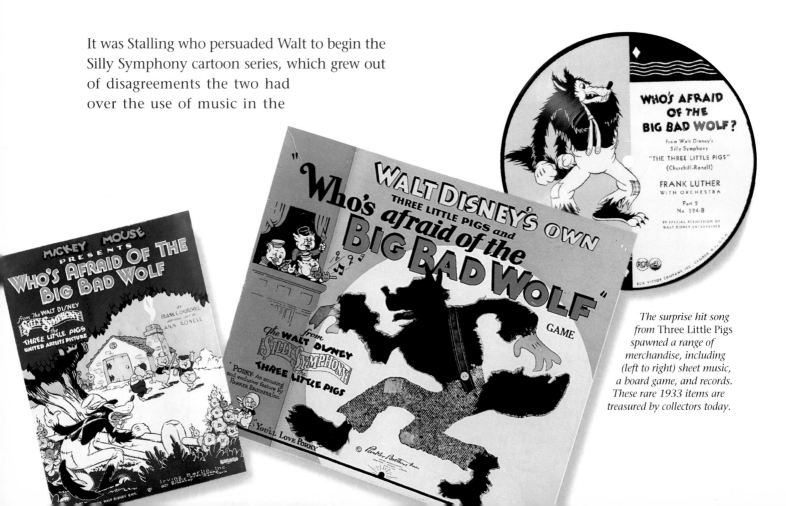

The surprise hit song from Three Little Pigs spawned a range of merchandise, including (left to right) sheet music, a board game, and records. These rare 1933 items are treasured by collectors today.

One of the composers he hired was Frank Churchill, a young musician who had studied at UCLA and gained experience playing honky-tonk piano in Mexico and peforming on a Los Angeles radio station (as well as serving as a session player in recording sessions for Disney cartoons). This heretofore unsung musician would play an important role in Disney music over the next decade. And he started off with a bang, writing Disney's first big hit, a song that came out of the most famous of the Silly Symphonies, *Three Little Pigs*.

Released in 1933 during the depths of the Depression, *Three Little Pigs* and its famous song, "Who's Afraid of the Big Bad Wolf?," provided hope and humor to a country that was badly in need of both.

As with many Disney films, *Three Little Pigs* comes from a children's story. But to Churchill, it also represented real life. While growing up on his family's ranch in San Luis Obispo, California, he was given three piglets to raise by his mother. All went well until a real "Big Bad Wolf" killed one of them.

As legend has it, when Churchill was asked to write a song for the cartoon, he recalled his horrifying childhood experience and penned "Who's Afraid of the Big Bad Wolf?" in about five minutes, patterning the song loosely on "Happy Birthday." When it was released as a single and in sheet music, it featured additional lyrics by Ann Ronell.

"Who's Afraid of the Big Bad Wolf?" provided hope and humor to a country that was badly in need of both.

With "Who's Afraid of the Big Bad Wolf?" Walt Disney and his staff had created their first sing-a-long classic. It certainly wasn't going to be their last.

In 1929, the Disney Studio's creative team included (standing from left) Johnny Cannon, Walt Disney, Bert Gillett, Ub Iwerks, Wilfred Jackson, Les Clark; (seated from left) Carl Stalling, Jack King and Ben Sharpsteen.

A COMING OF AGE

The next step for Walt and his staff was the creation of the first full-length animated feature. But Walt wasn't content to "just" create and produce a feature-length cartoon. He envisioned something more.

From its beginnings, *Snow White and the Seven Dwarfs* was planned around music. However, early attempts at songs did not satisfy Walt. He complained that they were too much in the vein of so many Hollywood musicals that introduced songs without regard to the story. "We should set a new pattern, a new way to use music," he told his staff. "Weave it into the story so somebody doesn't just burst into song."

That last line, as simply stated as it is, has been the guiding principle in Disney animated features from *Snow White* and *Pinocchio* all the way through the more recent efforts, including *Beauty and the Beast, Aladdin* and *The Lion King.*

What Walt wanted with *Snow White and the Seven Dwarfs* was something closer to Broadway musical than Hollywood motion picture.

Frank Churchill and Larry Morey were assigned the task of writing the songs for *Snow White.* By the time all was said and sung, the pair had written 25 songs, only eight of which ended up in the film. But what an eight they were, each one a classic in its own right.

The first original motion picture soundtrack record album was Snow White and the Seven Dwarfs, *released by Victor Records in 1937.*

"*We should set a new pattern, a new way to use music*"

Walt Disney didn't write any songs for *Snow White*, but he played an active role in defining the content of each song and how it would fit into the film, as these notes from a story conference on "Whistle While You Work" demonstrate:

> Change words of song so they fit in more with Snow White's handing the animals brushes, etc. Snow White: "If you just hum a merry tune"...and they start humming. Then Snow White would start to tell them to "whistle while you work." She would start giving the animals things to do. By that time, she has sung, of course... Birds would come marching in. Try to arrange to stay with the birds for a section of whistling. Orchestra would play with a whistling effect...get it in the woodwinds...like playing something instrumentally to sound like whistling...

> Get a way to finish the song that isn't just an end. Work in a shot trucking [moving] out of the house. Truck back and show animals shaking rugs out of the windows...little characters outside beating things out in the yard...

> Truck out and the melody of "Whistle While You Work" gets quieter and quieter. Leave them all working. The last thing you see as you truck away is little birds hanging out clothes. Fade out on that and music would fade out. At the end, all you would hear is the flute — before fading into the "Dig Dig" song [which precedes the song "Heigh-Ho"] and the hammering rhythm.

Snow White and the Seven Dwarfs ushered in not only the Golden Age of Disney Animation in the late 1930s and early 1940s, but the Golden Age of Disney Music as well. While Disney's animators were creating some of the most beautiful screen images ever seen, the studio's composers were producing some of the most memorable songs ever heard, including "When You Wish Upon a Star" from *Pinocchio* (1940), "Baby Mine" from *Dumbo* (1941) and "Little April Shower" from *Bambi* (1942).

World War II brought an abrupt end to the Golden Age. At the Disney Studios, the emphasis changed from creating animated features to producing cartoon shorts and instructional films to aid the war effort. Even after the war was over, Walt Disney didn't immediately return to animated features. Instead, he concentrated on "package" pictures (movies that featured a series of animated shorts rolled into one motion picture) and films featuring both live action and animation.

But Disney's staff of composers continued to play a significant role in these efforts, writing such memorable tunes as the Latin-influenced "Saludos Amigos" and "You Belong to My Heart" from the two South American travelog-style films *Saludos Amigos* (1943) and *The Three Caballeros* (1945), "The Lord Is Good to Me" from *Melody Time* (1948) and one of the most popular Disney songs ever written, "Zip-A-Dee-Doo-Dah," the irresistibly upbeat tune from *Song of the South* (1946).

Composer Frank Churchill (left) and sequence director/lyricist Larry Morey in the mid-1930s creating songs for Snow White and the Seven Dwarfs.

SONGS FROM TIN PAN ALLEY

In 1950, Walt Disney returned to animated features with the release of *Cinderella*, but instead of relying on his music staff for the film's song score, he turned to writers from New York's Tin Pan Alley, something he would continue to do for his animated features throughout the 1950s.

Originally 28th Street in Manhattan, Tin Pan Alley was home to many of the largest song publishers in the United States. Each publisher employed an army of songwriters, who worked out of small offices furnished with nothing more than pianos and music stands. During the summer, the writers would open their windows in a futile effort to get some relief from the stifling New York heat (the buildings weren't air conditioned). The noise of the pianos echoing through the street gave one the impression of people banging on tin pans, hence the name "Tin Pan Alley."

Walt didn't consciously set out to use Tin Pan Alley writers for *Cinderella*. While in New York on business prior to the start of production, he kept hearing on the radio a catchy novelty song, "Chi-Baba Chi-Baba," written by the team of Mack David, Jerry Livingston and Al Hoffman. He was so taken with the song that he ended up hiring the trio to write the songs for *Cinderella*. Perhaps it's no surprise, then, that one of the songs, "Bibbidi Bobbidi Boo," is in the same vein as "Chi-Baba."

Walt again turned to Tin Pan Alley for *Alice in Wonderland* (1951), primarily because he felt the film would need an abundance of novelty songs, something the Tin Pan Alley gang was quite adept at producing. In all, 14 songs were written for *Alice*, including "I'm Late," one of nine tunes written for the film by Bob Hilliard and Sammy Fain, and "The Unbirthday Song" contributed by the *Cinderella* trio of David, Hoffman and Livingston.

The renaissance in Disney animation continued through the 1950s and early 1960s with the release of such animated features as *Peter Pan* (1953), *Lady and the Tramp* (1955), *Sleeping Beauty* (1959) and *101 Dalmatians* (1961). The bulk of the songs continued to be written by Tin Pan Alley tunesmiths, such as Sammy Cahn, Sammy Fain and Jack Lawrence. The notable exception was *Lady and the Tramp*, which featured songs by Peggy Lee and Sonny Burke.

The increasing reliance on outside writers for songs for the animated features presented no danger to the jobs of Disney's crack staff of composers and arrangers. At least they didn't seem worried by it, perhaps because they were so busy.

[The 1950s were] a hectic time at the Studio," recalls Buddy Baker, who joined the Disney music staff following a career in big bands and radio, "We had the weekly series [*Disneyland*, which later became *The Wonderful World of Disney*, among other titles] to write music for, plus the daily show [*The Mickey Mouse Club*]. This was in addition to the feature films the Studio was producing. And Walt demanded quality, whether it was music for a multi-million dollar animated feature or a television show."

Walt's staff of composers was so busy writing the music they often turned to anyone who was ready, willing and able to write the lyrics, be they animators, scriptwriters, story editors or, in the case of "Old Yeller," Studio nurses (the lyrics for that song are credited to Gil George, who was in fact Disney Studio nurse Hazel George).

Disney staffers at the time included music director Oliver Wallace ("Old Yeller," and "Pretty Irish Girl"), Jimmie Dodd ("The Mickey Mouse March") and George Bruns ("Zorro" and "The Ballad of Davy Crockett").

Bruns' experience writing "The Ballad of Davy Crockett" for the *Davy Crockett* series of TV shows was typical of the way songs were written for Walt Disney in the harried '50s, though the results were far from typical.

"Walt needed what I call a little 'throwaway' tune that would bridge the time gaps in the story of Davy Crockett," recalled Bruns. "He needed a song that would carry the story from one sequence to another. I threw together the melody line and chorus, 'Davy, Davy Crockett, King of the Wild Frontier,' in about 30 minutes."

Tom Blackburn, the scriptwriter for the *Davy Crockett* series, had never before written a song, but that didn't stop him from adding the lyrics, 120 lines of them (the completed version has 20 stanzas of six lines each).

Even before the television series went on the air, "The Ballad of Davy Crockett" took the country by storm. Bruns and Blackburn's little "throwaway" tune became a national sensation, much as coonskin caps would when the show premiered.

"It certainly took everybody at the Studio by surprise," said Bruns. "The irony of it was that most people thought it was an authentic folk song that we had uncovered and updated. Usually when you have a hit song, there are always lawsuits claiming prior authorship. In the case of 'Davy Crockett,' not a single suit was filed."

"The Ballad of Davy Crockett" became the fastest-selling record of 1955.

Composer George Bruns created a diverse range of music for Disney, from the award-winning score for Sleeping Beauty *to the hit song "The Ballad of Davy Crockett."*

THE SHERMANS MARCH THROUGH DISNEY

If the 1950s were characterized by Walt Disney's reliance on Tin Pan Alley songwriters, the trend in the 1960s could be summed up in two words: Sherman Brothers.

Hired by Walt Disney in 1961 as staff songwriters, Richard M. and Robert B. Sherman proved versatile and prolific during their almost decade-long association with Disney, writing more than 200 songs, many of which have become timeless classics.

Perhaps the greatest achievement of the Sherman Brothers' Disney career came in 1964 with the release of *Mary Poppins*, for which they wrote 14 songs and earned two Academy Awards, one for Best Song ("Chim-Chim-Cher-ee") and the other for Best Song Score.

"Writing songs for *Mary Poppins* was a songwriter's dream. Each song we did had a purpose, a reason for being," says Robert Sherman, echoing the long-held philosophy of Walt Disney about music in motion pictures.

Typical of their experiences composing tunes for *Mary Poppins* was the inspiration behind one of the most popular and memorable tunes in the film, "Supercalifragilisticexpialidocious."

"When we were little boys in summer camp in the Catskill Mountains in the mid-1930s," explains Richard Sherman, "we heard this word. Not the exact word, but a word very similar to 'supercal.' It was a word that was longer than 'antidisestablishmentarianism,' and it gave us kids a word that no adult had. It was our own

"Supercalifragilisticexpialidocious"

The pair penned songs for animated features (*The Sword in the Stone* [1963], *The Jungle Book* [1967], *The Aristocats* [1970]) and featurettes (*Winnie the Pooh and the Honey Tree* [1966]), live-action musicals (*Summer Magic* [1963], *The Happiest Millionaire* [1967]), live-action non-musicals (*The Parent Trap* [1961], *In Search of the Castaways* [1962], *The Monkey's Uncle* [1965], *That Darn Cat* [1965]), musicals combining live-action and animation (*Bedknobs and Broomsticks* [1971]), theme parks (*The Enchanted Tiki Room* [1963]), and even the New York World's Fair (*Carousel of Progress*, *It's a Small World* [1964]).

special word, and we wanted the Banks children to have that same feeling."

Songwriters Richard Sherman (left) and Robert Sherman (right) review the music for Mary Poppins *with the film's co-producer and writer, Bill Walsh (center).*

*Dick Van Dyke,
Karen Dotrice,
Matthew Garber
and Julie Andrews
in Mary Poppins.*

Mary Poppins also proved to be the crowning achievement of Walt Disney's long and storied career. Combining live-action, animation and the Sherman Brothers song score, it was the culmination of everything he'd been working toward in his more than 40 years in the film business.

When Walt Disney passed away on December 15, 1966, there was concern that his studio would not be able to survive without him. But Walt had confidence it would. "I think by this time my staff…[is] convinced that Walt is right, that quality will out," he once said. "And so I think they're going to stay with that policy because it's proved that

it's a good business policy… I think they're convinced and I think they'll hang on, as you say, after Disney."

Throughout the 1970s and 1980s the Disney Studios continued producing animated and live-action features, but all of them, with the exceptions of *Robin Hood* (1973) and *Pete's Dragon* (1977), were non-musicals. That didn't mean there weren't *any* songs in Disney movies. Such animated features as *The Rescuers* (1977) and *The Fox and the Hound* (1981) did feature songs, but these songs were usually performed during the opening or closing credits and were not essential to the story.

A MUSICAL RENAISSANCE

"Animation is the last great place to do Broadway musicals," said Ashman, explaining the inspiration for *The Little Mermaid* (1989), *Beauty and the Beast* (1991) and *Aladdin* (1992). "It's a place you can use a whole other set of skills and a way of working which is more the way plays and musicals are made. With most films, the story seems to come first and the songs are an afterthought.

"Coming from a musical theater background," he continued, "Alan and I are used to writing songs for characters in situations. For *The Little Mermaid* we wanted songs that would really move the story forward and keep things driving ahead."

The seven songs Ashman and Menken wrote for the film did that and more. The result was the beginning of a New Golden Age of Animation that continues to this day.

Ashman and Menken followed the success of *The Little Mermaid* (for which they won an Academy Award for "Under the Sea") with *Beauty and the Beast*.

A review of the film in *Newsweek* magazine says it all: "The most delicious musical score of 1991 is Alan Menken and Howard Ashman's *Beauty and the Beast*. If the growing armada of

All that changed in 1988 with the release of *Oliver & Company*, Disney's first full-scale animated musical in more than a decade.

The film featured five tunes written by a Who's Who of pop songwriters, including Barry Manilow, Dan Hartman and Dean Pitchford. But the key was that all of the songs adhered to an old Disney maxim: music should play an integral and prominent part in the story without overshadowing or disrupting it.

"Music should come out of the dialogue," said the film's director, George Scribner, reemphasizing a point Walt Disney had made many times many years before. "The best

"Animation is the last great place to do Broadway musicals."

music advances the story or defines a character. The challenge was to figure out areas in our film where music could better express a concept or idea."

Perhaps no one knew this better than a New York-based lyricist named Howard Ashman, who co-wrote "Once Upon a Time in New York City" for *Oliver & Company*.

With his longtime writing partner Alan Menken, Ashman redefined and revitalized the animated musical, bringing to it a style, wit and sophistication that hadn't been seen or heard since the early 1940s.

titanically troubled Broadway musicals had half its charm and affectionate cleverness, the ships wouldn't be foundering."

The duo wrote six songs for the film, including an unprecedented three songs that were nominated for Academy Awards, "Be Our Guest" "Belle" and the eventual Oscar-winner "Beauty and the Beast."

Ariel and friends in The Little Mermaid.

The songwriting team of Howard Ashman (left) and Alan Menken received Academy Awards for their work on The Little Mermaid *and* Beauty and the Beast.

Before his death in March, 1991, Ashman had already begun work on *Aladdin*, and three of his songs (again written with his partner, Alan Menken) are heard in the film, including "Friend Like Me" and "Prince Ali."

Menken collaborated with Tim Rice (who, with Andrew Lloyd Webber, wrote *Jesus Christ Superstar* and *Evita*) on the remaining three songs in *Aladdin*, "One Jump Ahead," a reprise of "Prince Ali" and the Academy Award-winning "A Whole New World."

Walt Disney once said of Disneyland that it "will never be completed. It will continue to grow as long as there is imagination left in the world." He could just as easily have been talking about Disney music, for as long as there's imagination left in the world, people with musical dreams will continue adding to the beloved Disney library of song classics.

And, in fact, it's already happening. Buoyed by such songwriters as Alan Menken, Tim Rice, pop star Elton John, and famed lyricist Stephen Schwartz (*Godspell, Pippin*).

Rice has teamed with John to write songs for the upcoming animated feature *The Lion King*; and Menken is collaborating with Schwartz to create music for *Pocahontas*, Disney's 33rd full-length animated feature.

Members of the "Mickey Mouse Club" in a group shot with Walt Disney.

Perhaps it was Walt Disney himself who summed up best the reasons for the important role and the incredible success music has enjoyed in Disney animated features, live-action motion pictures and theme parks:

"Music has always had a prominent part in all our products from the early cartoon days. So much so, in fact, that I cannot think of the pictorial story without thinking about the complementary music that will fulfill it … I have had no formal musical training. But by long experience and by strong personal leaning, I've selected musical themes, original or adapted, that were guided to wide audience acceptance.

But credit for the memorable songs and scores must, of course, go to the brilliant composers and musicians who have been associated with me through the years."

Minnie's Yoo Hoo

From Walt Disney's *Mickey's Follies*

Words by WALT DISNEY and CARL STALLING
Music by CARL STALLING

Moderately

I'm the guy they call lit - tle Mick - ey Mouse, got a
blue bird down in the cher - ry tree, and the

sweet - ie down in the chick - en house, neith - er fat nor skin - ny, she's the
bu - sy buzz of the bum - ble bee, eve - ning bells a - ring - in', whip-poor-

hors - es whin - ny she's my lit - tle Min - nie mouse. When it's
wills a - sing - in' well they don't mean much to me. For my

24

Who's Afraid Of The Big Bad Wolf?

From Walt Disney's *Three Little Pigs*

Words and Music by FRANK CHURCHILL
Additional lyric by ANN RONELL

Who's a-fraid of the big bad wolf, big bad wolf, big bad wolf? Who's a-fraid of the big bad wolf? Tra la la la la. Who's a-fraid of the big bad wolf, big bad wolf, big bad wolf? Who's a-fraid of the big bad wolf? Tra la la la

Heigh-Ho

From Walt Disney's
Snow White And The Seven Dwarfs

Words by LARRY MOREY
Music by FRANK CHURCHILL

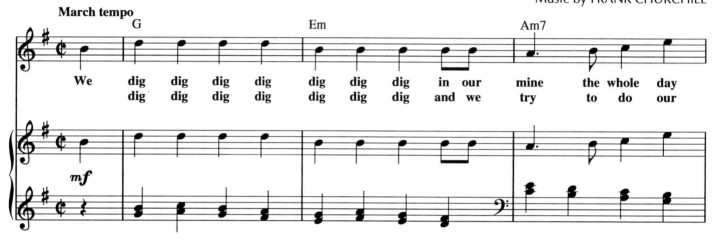

Some Day My Prince Will Come

From Walt Disney's
Snow White And The Seven Dwarfs

Words by LARRY MOREY
Music by FRANK CHURCHILL

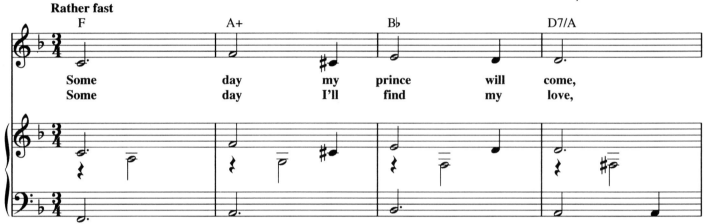

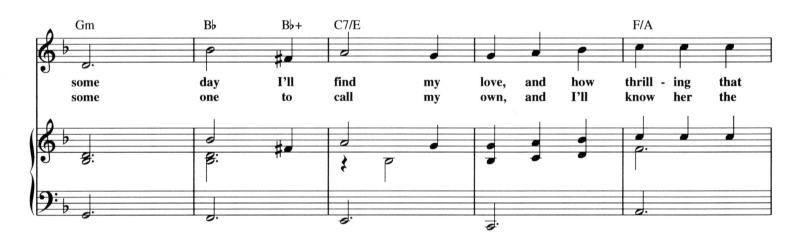

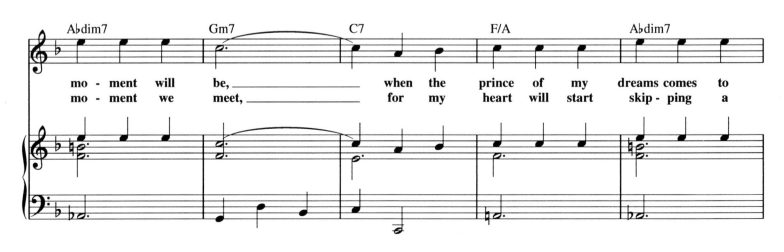

Whistle While You Work

From Walt Disney's
Snow White And The Seven Dwarfs

Words by LARRY MOREY
Music by FRANK CHURCHILL

Give A Little Whistle

From Walt Disney's *Pinocchio*

Words by NED WASHINGTON
Music by LEIGH HARLINE

When You Wish Upon A Star

From Walt Disney's *Pinocchio*

Words by NED WASHINGTON
Music by LEIGH HARLINE

Baby Mine

From Walt Disney's *Dumbo*

Words by NED WASHINGTON
Music by FRANK CHURCHILL

Moderately slow

Ba - by mine _____ don't you cry.

Ba - by mine _____ dry your eye.

Rest your head close to my heart, nev - er to part, ba - by of

Little April Shower

From Walt Disney's *Bambi*

Words by LARRY MOREY
Music by FRANK CHURCHILL

Lyrics:

Drip, drip, drop, lit-tle A-pril show-er, beat-ing a tune as you fall all a-round.
Drip, drip, drop, lit-tle A-pril show-er, beat-ing a tune ev-'ry-where that you fall.

Drip, drip, drop, lit-tle A-pril show-er, what can com-pare with your beau-ti-ful sound.
Drip, drip, drop, lit-tle A-pril show-er, I'm get-ting wet and I don't care at all.

Drip, drip, drop, when the sky is cloud-y

Love Is A Song

From Walt Disney's *Bambi*

Words by LARRY MOREY
Music by FRANK CHURCHILL

Moderately slow (with feeling)

Love is a song that nev - er ends.

Life may be swift and fleet - ing.

Hope may die, yet love's beau - ti - ful mu - sic

Zip-A-Dee-Doo-Dah
From Walt Disney's *Song Of The South*

Words by RAY GILBERT
Music by ALLIE WRUBEL

Moderately fast

Zip - a-dee doo - dah, zip - a-dee - ay. My, oh my, ___ what a won-der-ful day! ___ Plen - ty of sun- -shine, head - in' my way. ___ Zip - a-dee doo - dah,

The Lord Is Good To Me

From Walt Disney's *Johnny Appleseed*

Words and Music by KIM GANNON
and WALTER KENT

Lavender Blue
(Dilly Dilly)
From Walt Disney's *So Dear To My Heart*

Words by LARRY MOREY
Music by ELIOT DANIEL

61

A Dream Is A Wish Your Heart Makes

From Walt Disney's *Cinderella*

Words and Music by MACK DAVID,
AL HOFFMAN and JERRY LIVINGSTON

Moderately slow, with expression

A dream is a wish your heart makes ___

when you're fast a - sleep. ___ In dreams you will

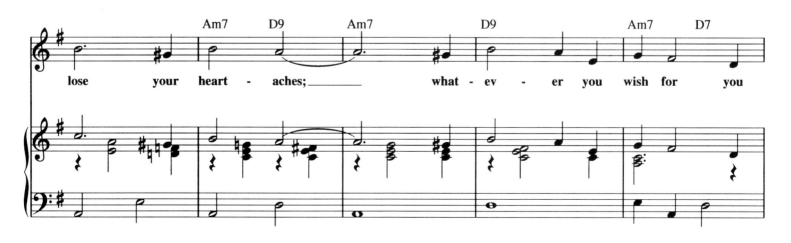

lose your heart - aches; ___ what - ev - er you wish for you

Bibbidi-Bobbidi-Boo
(The Magic Song)
From Walt Disney's *Cinderella*

Words by JERRY LIVINGSTON
Music by MACK DAVID and AL HOFFMAN

Sa - la - ga - doo - la men - chic - ka boo - la bib - bi - di - bob - bi - di - boo

put 'em to - geth - er and what have you got bib - bi - di - bob - bi - di - boo.

Sa - la - ga - doo - la men - chic - ka boo - la bib - bi - di - bob - bi - di - boo

So This Is Love
(The Cinderella Waltz)
From Walt Disney's *Cinderella*

Words and Music by MACK DAVID,
AL HOFFMAN and JERRY LIVINGSTON

I'm Late
From Walt Disney's *Alice In Wonderland*

Words by BOB HILLIARD
Music by SAMMY FAIN

The Unbirthday Song

From Walt Disney's *Alice In Wonderland*

Words and Music by MACK DAVID, AL HOFFMAN
and JERRY LIVINGSTON

The Second Star To The Right

From Walt Disney's *Peter Pan*

Words by SAMMY CAHN
Music by SAMMY FAIN

You Can Fly!
You Can Fly! You Can Fly!

From Walt Disney's *Peter Pan*

Words by SAMMY CAHN
Music by SAMMY FAIN

Moderately slow

Think of the pres-ents you're brought, an - y mer-ry lit - tle thought.

Think of Christ - mas, think of snow, think of sleigh bells, here we go! Like

rein-deer in the sky. _____ You can fly! You can

Bella Notte
From Walt Disney's *Lady And The Tramp*

Words and Music by PEGGY LEE
and SONNY BURKE

This __ is the night, __ it's a beau - ti - ful night __ and we call it bel - la

not - te. Look __ at the skies, __ they have stars __ in their eyes __ on this

love - ly bel - la not - te. So take the love ___ of your

Once Upon A Dream

From Walt Disney's *Sleeping Beauty*

Words and Music by SAMMY FAIN
and JACK LAWRENCE
Adapted From A Theme By Tchaikovsky

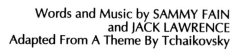

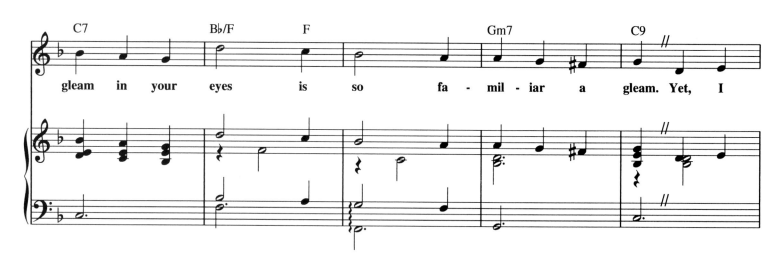

Cruella De Vil

From Walt Disney's
One Hundred And One Dalmations

Words and Music by
MEL LEVEN

Slow Blues

Cru - el - la De - Vil, __ Cru - el - la De - Vil, __ if she does-n't scare_ you no

ev - il thing will. __ To see her is to take a sud - den chill. _____ Cru-

el - la, Cru - el - la De - Vil. The curl of her lips, __ the

Higitus Figitus
(Merlin's Magic Song)
From Walt Disney's *The Sword In The Stone*

Words and Music by RICHARD M. SHERMAN
and ROBERT B. SHERMAN

Moderately

Hig - i - tus fig - i - tus zum - ba - ba - zing, I want your at - ten - tion ev - 'ry thing! We're

pack - ing to leave come on let's go, books are al - ways first you know.

Hock - e - ty pock - e - ty wock - e - ty wack, ab - ra - cab - ra dab - ra nack.

Chim Chim Cher-ee

From Walt Disney's *Mary Poppins*

Words and Music by RICHARD M. SHERMAN
and ROBERT B. SHERMAN

A Spoonful Of Sugar

From Walt Disney's *Mary Poppins*

Words and Music by RICHARD M. SHERMAN
and ROBERT B. SHERMAN

In ev-'ry job that must be done there is an el-e-ment of fun. You
feath-er-ing his nest has ver-y lit-tle time to rest while
bees that fetch the nec-tar from the flow-ers to the comb nev-er

find the fun and snap the job's a game._____ And ev-'ry task you un-der-
gath-er-ing his bits of twine and twig._____ Though quite in-tent in his pur-
tire of ev-er buzz-ing to and fro._____ Be-cause they take a lit-tle

take be-comes a piece of cake. A lark! A spree! It's
suit, he has a mer-ry tune to toot. He knows a song will
nip, from ev-'ry flow-er that they sip. And hence, they find their

102

Supercalifragilistic-expialidocious
From Walt Disney's *Mary Poppins*

Words and Music by RICHARD M. SHERMAN
and ROBERT B. SHERMAN

104

Winnie The Pooh

From Walt Disney's
Winnie The Pooh And The Honey Tree

Words and Music by RICHARD M. SHERMAN
and ROBERT B. SHERMAN

Broadly

Win - nie The Pooh, Win - nie The Pooh, tub - by lit - tle cub - by all stuffed with fluff. He's

Win - nie The Pooh, Win - nie The Pooh, wil - ly nil - ly sil - ly ole bear. Deep in the

hun - dred ac - re wood where Chris - to - pher Ro - bin plays,

The Wonderful Thing About Tiggers

From Walt Disney's
Winnie The Pooh And The Blustery Day

Words and Music by RICHARD M. SHERMAN
and ROBERT B. SHERMAN

The Bare Necessities

From Walt Disney's *The Jungle Book*

Words and Music by
TERRY GILKYSON

Look for the 1.,3. bare ne - ces - si - ties, the sim - ple bare ne -
2. bare ne - ces - si - ties, the sim - ple bare ne -

ces - si - ties;___ for - get a - bout your wor - ries and your strife.
ces - si - ties;___ for - get a - bout your wor - ries and your strife.

I mean the bare ne - ces - si - ties,___ or Moth - er Na - ture's
I mean the bare ne - ces - si - ties,___ that's why a bear can

I Wan'na Be Like You
(The Monkey Song)
From Walt Disney's *The Jungle Book*

Words and Music by RICHARD M. SHERMAN
and ROBERT B. SHERMAN

Trust In Me

From Walt Disney's *The Jungle Book*

Words and Music by RICHARD M. SHERMAN
and ROBERT B. SHERMAN

Lyrics:
Trust in me, _____ just in me. _____ Shut your eyes _____ and trust in me. _____ You can sleep _____ safe and sound _____ know-ing

Ev'rybody Wants To Be A Cat

From Walt Disney's *The Aristocats*

Words by FLOYD HUDDLESTON
Music by AL RINKER

The Aristocats

From Walt Disney's *The Aristocats*

Words and Music by RICHARD M. SHERMAN
and ROBERT B. SHERMAN

Brightly

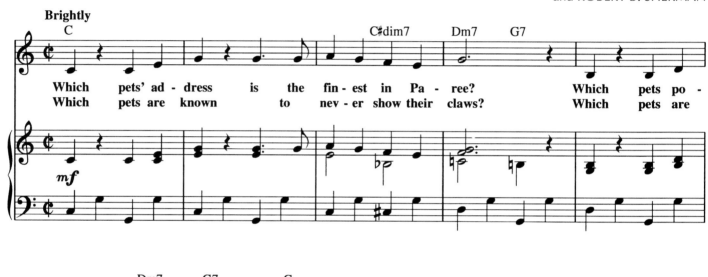

Which pets' ad - dress is the fin - est in Pa - ree? Which pets po -
Which pets are known to nev - er show their claws? Which pets are

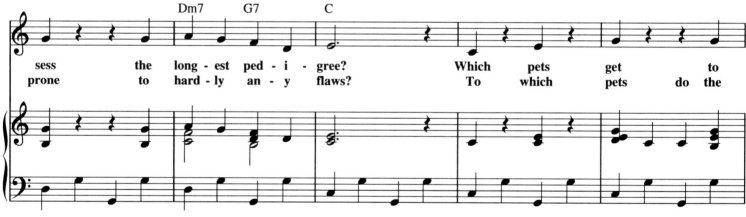

sess the long - est ped - i - gree? Which pets get to
prone to hard - ly an - y flaws? To pets which pets do the

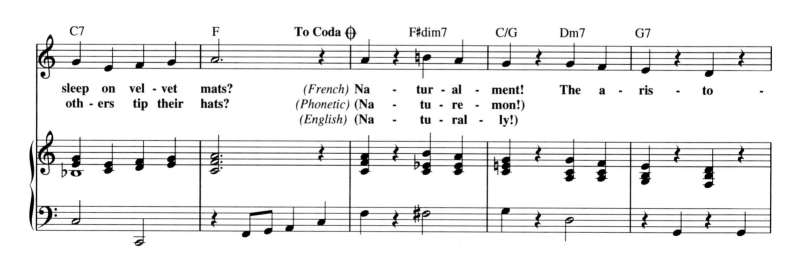

sleep on vel - vet mats? (French) Na - tur - al - ment! The a - ris - to -
oth - ers tip their hats? (Phonetic) (Na - tu - re - mon!)
(English) (Na - tu - ral - ly!)

The Age Of Not Believing

From Walt Disney's *Bedknobs And Broomsticks*

Words and Music by RICHARD M. SHERMAN
and ROBERT B. SHERMAN

Oo-De-Lally

From Walt Disney's *Robin Hood*

Words and Music by
ROGER MILLER

Rob - in Hood and Lit - tle John walk - in' thru the for - est, laugh-in' back and forth at what the
Rob - in Hood and Lit - tle John run-nin' thru the for - est, jump-in' fen - ces dodg-in' trees and

oth-er 'un has to say. Rem - i - nisc - in' this 'n that 'n
try-in' to get a - way. Con-tem-plat-in' noth-in' but es -

hav - in' such a good time. Oo - de - lal - ly, Hoo - de - lal - ly, gol - ly what a day!
cape and fin - 'ly makin' it.

Someone's Waiting For You

From Walt Disney's *The Rescuers*

Words by CAROL CONNORS and AYN ROBBINS
Music by SAMMY FAIN

Candle On The Water

From Walt Disney's *Pete's Dragon*

Words and Music by AL KASHA
and JOEL HIRSCHHORN

I'll be your can-dle on the wa-ter, my love for you will al-ways burn.

I'll be your can-dle on the wa-ter, 'til ev-'ry wave is warm and bright,

I know you're lost and drift-ing, but the clouds are lift-ing,

my soul is there be-side you, let this can-dle guide you

don't give up you have some-where to turn.

soon you'll see a gold-en stream of light.

Best Of Friends

From Walt Disney's *The Fox And The Hound*

Words by STAN FIDEL
Music by RICHARD JOHNSTON

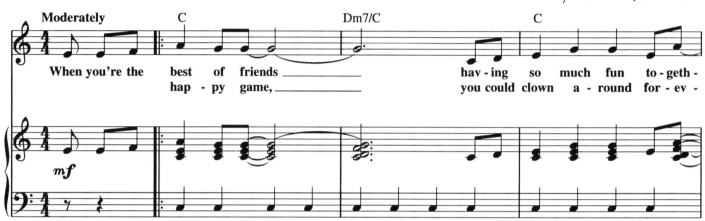

Once Upon A Time In New York City

From Walt Disney's *Oliver & Company*

Words by HOWARD ASHMAN
Music by BARRY MANN

Moderately

Now it's al - ways once up - on a time ___ in New York Cit - y.

It's a big old, bad ___ old, tough ___ old town, ___ it's true. ___

But be - gin - nings are ___ con - ta - gious there, ___ they're al - ways set - ting

Perfect Isn't Easy

From Walt Disney's *Oliver & Company*

Words by JACK FELDMAN
and BRUCE SUSSMAN
Music by BARRY MANILOW

Girls, we've got work to do. ___ Pass me the paint and glue.

Per - fect is - n't eas - y but it's me. ___ When one knows the

world is watch - ing, one does what one must. Some mi - nor ad - just-ments, dar - ling;

Kiss The Girl

From Walt Disney's *The Little Mermaid*

Lyrics by HOWARD ASHMAN
Music by ALAN MENKEN

Moderately

There you see __ her ___ sit- ting there a- cross the way. ___

She don't got a lot to say, ___ but there's some-thing a- bout her.

Kiss The Girl

From Walt Disney's *The Little Mermaid*

Lyrics by Howard Ashman
Music by Alan Menken

There you see her sitting there across the way.
She don't got a lot to say, but there's something about her.
And you don't know why, but you're dying to try.
You wanna kiss the girl.
Yes, you want her.
Look at her, you know you do.
Possible she wants you, too.
There is one way to ask her.
It don't take a word, not a single word, go on and kiss the girl.
Sha la la la la la, my oh my,
Look like the boy too shy.
Ain't gonna kiss the girl.
Sha la la la la la, ain't that sad.
Ain't it a shame, too bad.
He gonna miss the girl.
Now's your moment, floating in a blue lagoon.
Boy, you better do it soon, no time will be better.
She don't say a word and she won't say a word until you kiss the girl.
Sha la la la la la, don't be scared.
You got the mood prepared, go on and kiss the girl.
Sha la la la la la, don't stop now.
Don't try to hide it how
You wanna kiss the girl. Sha la la la la la, float along.
And listen to the song, the song say kiss the girl.
Sha la la la la the music play.
Do what the music say.
You gotta kiss the girl.
You've got to kiss the girl.
You wanna kiss the girl.
You've gotta kiss the girl.
Go on and kiss the girl.

Part Of Your World

From Walt Disney's *The Little Mermaid*

Lyrics by HOWARD ASHMAN
Music by ALAN MENKEN

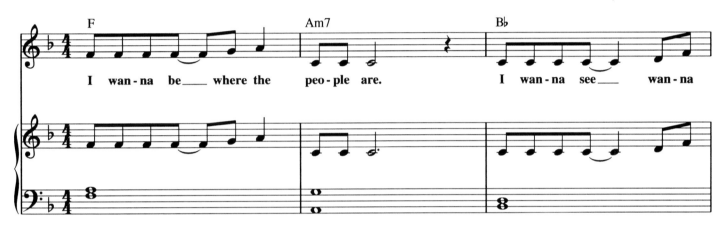

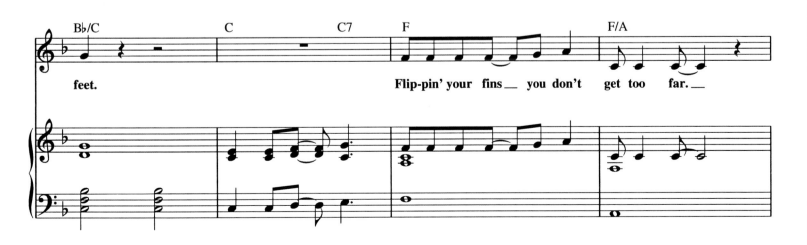

Part Of Your World
From Walt Disney's *The Little Mermaid*

Lyrics by Howard Ashman
Music by Alan Menken

Look at this stuff.
Isn't it neat?
Wouldn't you think my collection's complete?
Wouldn't you think I'm the girl, the girl who has ev'rything.
Look at this trove, treasures untold.
How many wonders can one cavern hold?
Looking around here you'd think, sure, she's got ev'rything.
I've got gadgets and gizmos aplenty.
I've got whozits and whatzits galore.
You want thingamabobs, I've got twenty.
But who cares?
No big deal. I want more.
I wanna be where the people are.
I wanna see wanna see 'em dancin',
Walkin' around on those, whatdya call 'em, oh feet.
Flippin' your fins you don't get too far.
Legs are required for jumpin', dancin'.
Strollin' along down the, what's that word again, street.
Up where they walk, up where they run, up where they stay all day in the sun.
Wanderin' free, wish I could be part of that world.
What would I give if I could live outta these waters.
What would I pay to spend a day warm on the sand.
Betcha on land they understand.
Bet they don't reprimand their daughters.
Bright young women, sick of swimmin', ready to stand.
And ready to know what the people know.
Ask 'em my questions and get some answers.
What's a fire and why does it, what's the word, burn.
When's it my turn?
Wouldn't I love, love to explore that shore up above, out of the sea.
Wish I could be part of that world.

Under The Sea
From Walt Disney's *The Little Mermaid*

Lyrics by HOWARD ASHMAN
Music by ALAN MENKEN

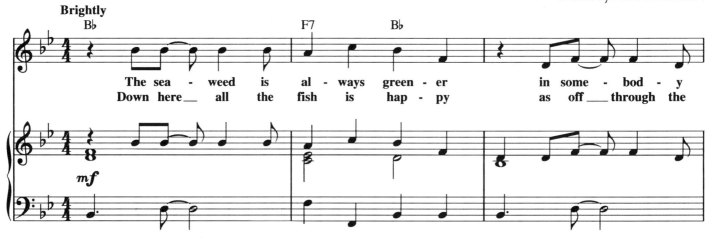

The sea - weed is al - ways green - er in some - bod - y
Down here _ all the fish is hap - py as off _ through the

else - 's lake. You dream _ a - bout go - ing up there.
waves dey roll. The fish _ on the land ain't hap - py.

But that _ is a big mis - take. Just look _ at the
They sad _ 'cause they in the bowl. But fish _ in the

Under The Sea
From Walt Disney's *The Little Mermaid*

Lyrics by Howard Ashman
Music by Alan Menken

The seaweed is always greener in somebody else's lake.
You dream about going up there.
But that is a big mistake.
Just look at the world around you, right here on the ocean floor.
Such wonderful things surround you.
What more is you lookin' for?
Under the sea, under the sea.
Darlin' it's better down where it's wetter.
Take it from me.
Up on the shore they work all day.
Out in the sun they slave away.
While we devotin' full time to floatin' under the sea.
Down here all the fish is happy as off through the waves they roll.
The fish on the land ain't happy.
They sad 'cause they in the bowl.
But fish in the bowl is lucky, they in for a worser fate.
One day when the boss get hungry guess who gon' be on the plate.
Under the sea, under the sea.
Nobody beat us, fry us and eat us in fricassee.
We what the land folks loves to cook.
Under the sea we off the hook.
We got no troubles life is the bubbles under the sea.
Under the sea.
Since life is sweet here we got the beat here naturally.
Even the sturgeon an' the ray they get the urge 'n' start to play.
We got the spirit, you got to hear it under the sea.
The newt play the flute.
The carp play the harp.
The plaice play the bass.
And they soundin' sharp.
The bass play the brass.
The chub play the tub.
The fluke is the duke of soul.
The ray he can play.
The lings on the strings.
The trout rockin' out.
The blackfish she sings.
The smelt and the sprat they know where it's at.
An' oh, that blowfish blow.
Under the sea.
Under the sea.
When the sardine begin the beguine it's music to me.
What do they got, a lot of sand.
We got a hot crustacean band.
Each little clam here know how to jam here under the sea.
Each little slug here cuttin' a rug here under the sea.
Each little snail here know how to wail here.
That's why it's hotter under the water.
Ya we in luck here down in the muck here under the sea.

Be Our Guest

From Walt Disney's *Beauty And The Beast*

Words by HOWARD ASHMAN
Music by ALAN MENKEN

Be our guest! Be our guest! Put our ser - vice to the

test. Tie your nap - kin 'round your neck, che - rie and we pro - vide the

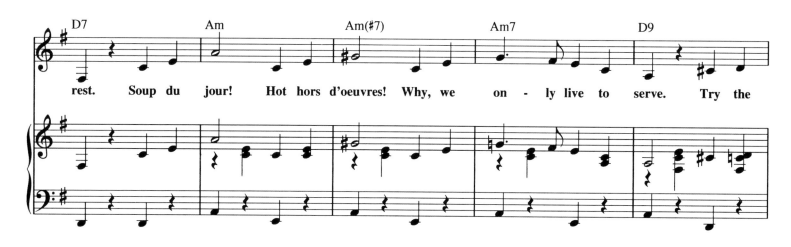

rest. Soup du jour! Hot hors d'oeuvres! Why, we on - ly live to serve. Try the

Be Our Guest

From Walt Disney's *Beauty And The Beast*

Lyrics by Howard Ashman
Music by Alan Menken

Lumiere:	Ma chere Mademoiselle, It is with deepest pride and greatest pleasure that we welcome you tonight. And now, we invite you to relax. Let us pull up a chair as the dining room proudly presents your dinner!
	Be our guest! Be our guest! Put our service to the test.
	Tie your napkin 'round your neck, cherie, And we provide the rest. Soup du jour! Hot hors d'oeuvres!
	Why, we only live to serve. Try the grey stuff, it's delicious! Don't believe me? Ask the dishes!
	They can sing! They can dance! After all, Miss, this is France! And a dinner here is never second best.
	Go on, unfold your menu, Take a glance, And then you'll be our guest, Oui, our guest! Be our guest!
	Beef ragout! Cheese souffle! Pie and pudding "en flambe!" We'll prepare and serve with flair A culinary cabaret!
	You're alone and you're scared But the banquet's all prepared. No one's gloomy or complaining While the flatware's entertaining.
	We tell jokes. I do tricks with my fellow candlesticks.
Mugs:	And it's all in perfect taste. That you can bet!
All:	Come on and lift your glass You've won your own free pass To be our guest!
Lumeniere:	If you're stressed, It's fine dining we suggest.
All:	Be our guest! Be our guest! Be our guest!
Lumeniere:	Life is so unnerving for a servant who's not serving. He's not whole without a soul to wait upon. Ah, those good old days when we were useful. Suddenly, those good old days are gone.

Ten years, we've been rusting,
Needing so much more — than dusting.
Needing exercise, a chance to use our skills.

Most days, we just lay around the castle.
Flabby, fat and lazy.
You walked in and oops-a-daisy.

Mrs. Potts: It's a guest!
It's a guest!
Sakes alive,
Well, I'll be blessed!

Wine's been poured and thank the Lord
I've had the napkins freshly pressed.
With dessert she'll want tea.

And my dear, that's fine with me.
While the cups do their soft shoeing,
I'll be bubbling!
I'll be brewing!

I'll get warm, piping hot!
Heaven's sakes!
Is that a spot?
Clean it up!

We want the company impressed!
We've got a lot to do.
Is it one lump or two
For you, our guest?

Chorus: She's our guest!

Mrs. Potts: She's our guest!

Chorus: She's our guest!
Be our guest!
Be our guest!

Our command is your request.
It's ten years since we had anybody here,
And we're obsessed.

With your meal
With your ease,
Yes, indeed,
We aim to please.

While the candlelight's still glowing
Let us help you,
We'll keep going.

Course by course,
One by one!
'Til you shout,
"Enough. I'm done!"

Then we'll sing you off to sleep as you digest.
Tonight you'll prop your feet up!
But for now, let's eat up!

Be our guest!
Be our guest!
Be our guest!
Please, be our guest!

Beauty And The Beast

From Walt Disney's *Beauty And The Beast*

Words by HOWARD ASHMAN
Music by ALAN MENKEN

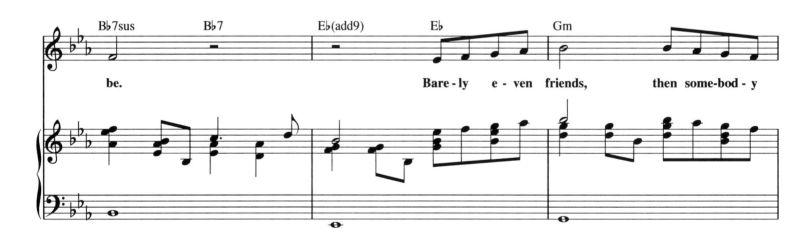

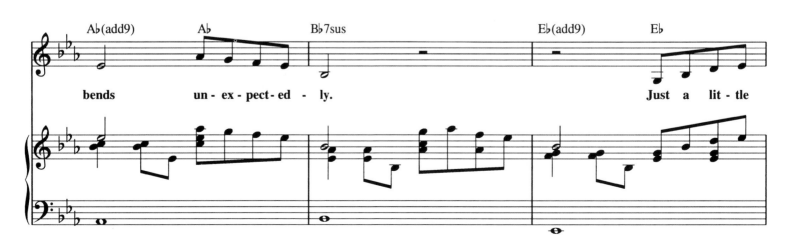

Beauty And The Beast

From Walt Disney's *Beauty And The Beast*

Lyrics by Howard Ashman
Music by Alan Menken

Tale as old as time,
True as it can be.
Barely even friends,
Then somebody bends
Unexpectedly.
Just a little change.
Small to say the least.
Both a little scared,
Neither one prepared.
Beauty and the Beast.
Ever just the same.
Ever a surprise.
Ever as before,
Ever just as sure
As the sun will rise.
Tale as old as time.
Tune as old as song.
Bittersweet and strange,
Finding you can change,
Learning you were wrong.
Certain as the sun
Rising in the East.
Tale as old as time,
Song as old as rhyme.
Beauty and the Beast.
Tale as old as time,
Song as old as rhyme.
Beauty and the Beast.

Belle

From Walt Disney's *Beauty And The Beast*

Words by HOWARD ASHMAN
Music by ALAN MENKEN

Moderately fast

C(add9) · G · C · G

Belle: There goes the bak - er with his tray, like
Townsfolk: Look there she goes that girl is strange, no
Townsfolk: Look there she goes that girl is so pe -

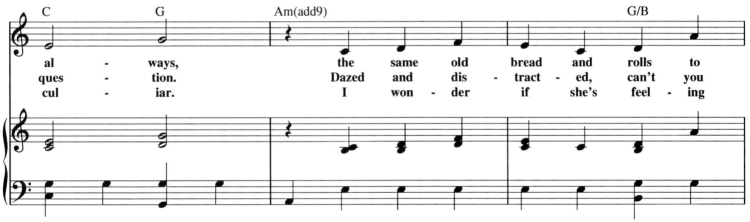

C · G · Am(add9) · G/B

al - ways,
ques - tion.
cul - iar.

the same old bread and rolls to
Dazed and dis - tract - ed, can't you
I won - der if she's feel - ing

C · Eb(add9) · F

sell.
tell?
well.

Ev - 'ry morn - ing just the
Nev - er part of an - y
With a dream - y, far - off

Belle
From Walt Disney's *Beauty And The Beast*

Lyrics by Howard Ashman
Music by Alan Menken

Belle:	Little town, it's a quiet village. Ev'ry day like the one before. Little town full of little people Waking up to say:
Townsfolk:	Bonjour! Bonjour! Bonjour! Bonjour! Bonjour!
Belle:	There goes the baker with his tray, like always, The same old bread and rolls to sell. Ev'ry morning just the same Since the morning that we came To this poor provincial town.
Baker:	Good Morning, Belle!
Belle:	Morning, Monsieur.
Baker:	Where are you off to?
Belle:	The bookshop. I just finished the most wonderful story about a beanstalk and an ogre and a...
Baker:	That's nice. Marie! The baguettes! Hurry up!
Townsfolk:	Look there she goes that girl is strange, no question. Dazed and distracted, can't you tell? Never part of any crowd, 'Cause her head's up on some cloud. No denying she's a funny girl, that Belle.
Man I:	Bonjour.
Woman I:	Good day.
Man I:	How is your fam'ly?
Woman II:	Bonjour.
Man II:	Good day.
Woman II:	How is your wife?
Woman III:	I need six eggs!
Man III:	That's too expensive.
Belle:	There must be more than this provincial life.
Bookseller:	Ah, Belle!
Belle:	Good morning. I've come to return the book I borrowed.
Bookseller:	Finished already?
Belle:	Oh, I couldn't put it down. Have you got anything new?
Bookseller:	Ha, ha! Not since yesterday.
Belle:	That's alright. I'll borrow this one!
Bookseller:	That one? But you've read it twice!
Belle:	Well, it's my favorite! Far off places, daring sword fights, Magic spells, a prince in disguise...

Bookseller:	If you like it all that much, it's yours!
Belle:	But sir!
Bookseller:	I insist.
Belle:	Well, thank you. Thank you very much!
Townsfolk:	Look there she goes that girl is so peculiar. I wonder if she's feeling well. With a dreamy, far-off look And her nose stuck in a book, What a puzzle to the rest of us is Belle.
Belle:	Oh, isn't this amazing? It's my fav'rite part because you'll see. Here's where she meets Prince Charming But she won't discover that it's him 'til chapter three.
Woman:	Now, it's no wonder that her name means "beauty." Her looks have got no parallel.
Shopkeeper:	But behind that fair facade. I'm afraid she's rather odd. Very diff'rent from the rest of us.
Townsfolk:	She's nothing like the rest of us. Yes, diff'rent from the rest of us is Belle.
Gaston:	Right from the moment when I met her, saw her, I said she's gorgeous and I fell. Here in town there's only she who is beautiful as me, I'm making plans to woo and marry Belle.
Silly Girls:	Look there he goes! Isn't he dreamy? Monsieur Gaston! Oh, he's so cute! Be still my heart! I'm hardly breathing! He's such a tall, dark, strong and handsome brute.
Man I:	Bonjour!
Man II:	Good day.
Matron:	You call this bacon?
Man IV:	Some cheese... ...One pound.
Cheese Merchant:	I'll get the knife.
Woman I:	This bread... ...It's stale!
Baker:	Madame's mistaken.
Belle:	There must be more than this provincial life!
Gaston:	Just watch I'm going to make Belle my wife!
Townsfolk:	Look there she goes a girl who's strange but special. A most peculiar mad'moiselle. It's a pity and a sin. She doesn't quite fit in 'Cause she really is a funny girl A beauty but a funny girl. She really is a funny girl That Belle!

Gaston

From Walt Disney's *Beauty And The Beast*

Words by HOWARD ASHMAN
Music by ALAN MENKEN

Gaston

From Walt Disney's *Beauty And The Beast*

Lyrics by Howard Ashman
Music by Alan Menken

Gaston:	Who does she think she is? That girl has tangled with the wrong man! No one says "no" to Gaston!
LeFou:	Heh, Heh. Darn right.
Gaston:	Dismissed! Rejected! Publicly humiliated! Why it's more than I can bear.
LeFou:	More beer?
Gaston:	What for? Nothing helps. I'm disgraced.
LeFou:	Who, you? Never! Gaston, you've got to pull yourself together.
LeFou:	Gosh it disturbs me to see you, Gaston, Looking so down in the dumps. Ev'ry guy here'd love to be you, Gaston, Even when taking your lumps. There's no man in town as admired as you You're everyone's favorite guy. Ev'ryone's awed and inspired by you, And it's not very hard to see why. No one's slick as Gaston. No one's quick as Gaston. No one's neck's as incredibly thick as Gaston! For there's no man in town half as manly. Perfect! A pure paragon! You can ask any Tom, Dick, or Stanley And they'll tell you whose team they prefer to be on!
Chorus:	No one's been like Gaston, A kingpin like Gaston.
LeFou:	No one's got a swell cleft in his chin like Gaston!
Gaston:	As a specimen, yes, I'm intimidating!
Chorus:	My, what a guy, that Gaston! Give five "hurrahs!" Give twelve "hip-hips!"
LeFou:	Gaston is the best and the rest is all drips!
Chorus:	No one fights like Gaston, douses lights like Gaston.
Cronie:	In a wrestling match, nobody bites like Gaston!

Girls:	For there's no one as burly and brawny.
Gaston:	As you see, I've got biceps to spare.
LeFou:	Not a bit of him's scraggly or scrawny
Gaston:	That's right! And ev'ry last inch of me's covered with hair!
Cronies:	No one hits like Gaston,
Townsmen:	Matches wits like Gaston
LeFou:	In a spitting match nobody spits like Gaston.
Gaston:	I'm especially good at expectorating! Ptooey!
Chorus:	Ten points for Gaston!
Gaston:	When I was a lad, I ate four dozen eggs ev'ry morning to help me get large. And now that I'm grown I eat five dozen eggs, So I'm roughly the size of a barge.
Chorus:	No one shoots like Gaston, Makes those beauts like Gaston.
LeFou:	Then goes tromping around wearing boots like Gaston.
Gaston:	I use antlers in all of my decorating! Say it again. Who's a man among men? And then say it once more. Who's the hero next door? Who's a super success? Don't you know? Can't you guess? Ask his fans and his five hangers on. There's just one guy in town who's got all of it down.
LeFou:	And his name's G-A-S-T-G-A-S-T-E-G-A-S-T-O-oh oh!
Chorus:	Gaston.

Friend Like Me

From Walt Disney's *Aladdin*

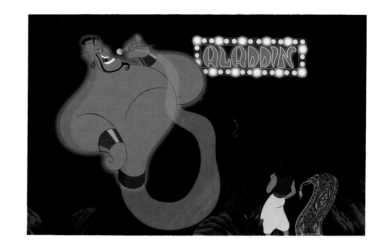

Words by HOWARD ASHMAN
Music by ALAN MENKEN

Bright two-beat
GENIE:

Well A - li Ba - ba had them for - ty thieves. Sche-her - a - za - de had a thou-sand tales. _

But, mas - ter, you in luck 'cause up your sleeves_ you got a

brand of mag - ic nev - er fails. _ You got some pow - er in your

Friend Like Me

From Walt Disney's *Aladdin*

Lyrics by Howard Ashman
Music by Alan Menken

Genie:

Well, Ali Baba had them forty thieves.
Scheherazade had a thousand tales.
But, master, you in luck 'cause up your sleeves
You got a brand of magic never fails.
You got some power in your corner now,
Some heavy ammunition in your camp.
You got some punch, pizazz, yahoo and how.
See, all you gotta do is rub that lamp.
And I'll say, Mister Aladdin, sir,
What will your pleasure be?
Let me take your order, jot it down.
You ain't never had a friend like me. No no no.
Life is your restaurant and I'm your maitre d'.
C'mon whisper what it is you want.
You ain't never had a friend like me.
Yes sir, we pride ourselves on service.
You're the boss, the king, the shah.
Say what you wish. It's yours!
True dish, how 'bout a little more baklava?
Have some of column "A".
Try all of column "B".
I'm in the mood to help you, dude,
You ain't never had a friend like me.
Wa-ah-ah. Oh my.
Wa-ah-ah. No no.
Wah-ah-ah. Na na na.
Can your friends do this?
Can your friends do that?
Can your friends pull this out their little hat?
Can your friends go poof!
(Spoken:) *Well, looky here.*
Can your friends go abracadabra,
Let 'er rip and then make the sucker disappear?
So doncha sit there slack jawed, buggy eyed.
I'm here to answer all your midday prayers.
You got me bonafide certified.
You got a genie for your chargé d'affaires.
I got a powerful urge to help you out.
So whatcha wish I really want to know.
You got a list that's three miles long, no doubt.
Well, all you gotta do is rub like so. And oh.
Mister Aladdin, sir, have a wish or two or three.
I'm on the job, you big nabob.
You ain't never had a friend, never had a friend,
You ain't never had a friend, never had a friend.
You ain't never had a friend like me.
Wa-ah-ah. Wa-ah-ah.
You ain't never had a friend like me. Ha!

One Jump Ahead

From Walt Disney's *Aladdin*

Music by ALAN MENKEN
Lyrics by TIM RICE

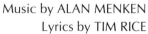

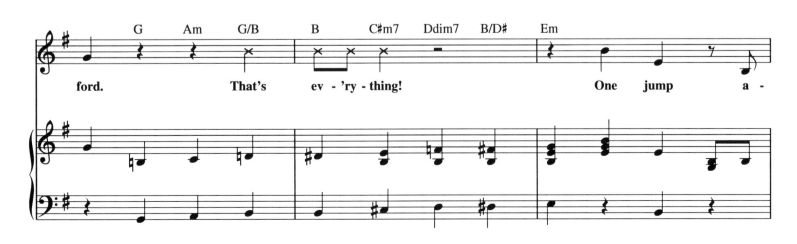

One Jump Ahead

From Walt Disney's *Aladdin*

Music by Alan Menken
Words by Tim Rice

Aladdin:	Gotta keep one jump ahead of the breadline,
	One swing ahead of the sword.
	I steal only what I can't afford.
	(Spoken:) *That's everything!*
	One jump ahead of the lawmen.
	That's all, and that's no joke.
	These guys don't appreciate I'm broke.
Crowd:	Riff raff! Street rat! Scoundrel! Take that!
Aladdin:	Just a little snack, guys.
Crowd:	Rip him open, take it back, guys.
Aladdin:	I can take a hint, gotta face the facts.
	You're my only friend, Abu!
Crowd:	Who?
Ladies:	Oh it's sad Aladdin's hit the bottom.
	He's become a one man rise in crime.
	I'd blame parents except he hasn't got 'em.
Aladdin:	Gotta eat to live, gotta steal to eat,
	Tell you all about it when I got the time!
	One jump ahead of the slowpokes,
	One skip ahead of my doom.
	Next time gonna use a nom-de-plume.
	One jump ahead of the hitmen,
	One hit ahead of the flock.
	I think I'll take a stroll around the block.
Crowd:	Stop thief! Vandal! Outrage! Scandal!
Aladdin:	Let's not be too hasty.
Lady:	Still I think he's rather tasty.
Aladdin:	Gotta eat to live, gotta steal to eat,
	Otherwise we'd get along.
Crowd:	(Spoken:) *Wrong!*
Aladdin:	One jump ahead of the hoofbeats.
Crowd:	Vandal!
Aladdin:	One hop ahead of the hump.
Crowd:	Streetrat!
Aladdin:	One trick ahead of disaster.
Crowd:	Scoundrel!
Aladdin:	They're quick but I'm much faster.
Crowd:	Take that!
Aladdin:	Here goes. Better throw my hand in.
	Wish me happy landin'.
	All I gotta do is jump!

194

Prince Ali

From Walt Disney's *Aladdin*

Words by HOWARD ASHMAN
Music by ALAN MENKEN

Prince Ali
From Walt Disney's *Aladdin*

Words by Howard Ashman
Music by Alan Menken

Chorus:	Make way for Prince Ali.
	Say hey, it's Prince Ali.
Genie:	Hey! Clear the way in the old Bazaar.
	Hey you! Let us through!
	It's a bright new star!
	Oh, come be the first on your block
	To meet his eye.
	Make way, here he comes!
	Ring bells. Bang the drums!
	Are you gonna love this guy!
	Prince Ali! Fabulous he! Ali Ababwa.
	Genuflect. Show some respect.
	Down on one knee!
	Now try your best to stay calm.
	Brush up your Sunday salaam.
	Then come and meet his spectacular coterie.
	Prince Ali! Mighty is he! Ali Ababwa.
	Strong as ten regular men definitely.
	He faced the galloping hordes,
	A hundred bad guys with swords.
	Who sent those goons to their Lords?
	Why, Prince Ali.
Chorus:	He's got seventy-five golden camels.
Genie:	(Spoken:) *Don't they look lovely, June?*
Chorus:	Purple peacocks, he's got fifty-three.
Genie:	(Spoken:) *Fabulous, Harry, I love the feathers.*
Chorus:	When it comes to exotic type mammals,
	Has he got a zoo?
	I'm telling you, it's a world class menagerie.
Genie:	Prince Ali, handsome is he,
Chorus:	There's no question this Ali's alluring.
Genie:	Ali Ababwa.
Chorus:	Never ordinary, never boring.
Genie:	That physique! How can I speak?
	Weak at the knee.
Chorus:	Ev'rything about the man just plain impresses.
Genie:	Well, get on out in that square.
Chorus:	He's a winner, he's a whiz, a wonder.
Genie:	Adjust your veil and prepare
Chorus:	He's about to pull my heart asunder.
Genie:	To gawk and grovel and stare at Prince Ali.
Chorus:	And I absolutely love the way he dresses.
	He's got ninety-five white Persian monkeys.
	He's got the monkeys. Let's see the monkeys.
	And to view them he charges no fee.
	He's generous. So generous.
	He's got slaves, he's got servants and flunkies.
	Proud to work for him, bow to his whim,
	Love serving him.
	They're just lousy with loyalty to Ali!
	Prince Ali!
Chorus & Genie:	Prince Ali! Amorous he! Ali Ababwa.
Genie:	Hear your princess was a sight lovely to see.
	And that, good people, is why he got dolled up
	And dropped by
Chorus:	With sixty elephants, llamas galore,
	With his bears and lions, a brass band and more.
	With his forty fakirs, his cooks, his bakers,
	His birds that warble on key.
	Make way for Prince Ali!

A Whole New World

From Walt Disney's *Aladdin*

Music by ALAN MENKEN
Lyrics by TIM RICE

Sweetly

ALADDIN:

I can show you the world, shin-ing, shim-mer-ing, splen-did. Tell me prin-cess, now when did you last let your heart de-cide? I can o-pen your

A Whole New World
From Walt Disney's *Aladdin*

Music by Alan Menken
Words by Tim Rice

Aladdin:	I can show you the world,
	Shining, shimmering, splendid.
	Tell me princess, now
	When did you last let your heart decide?
	I can open your eyes
	Take you wonder by wonder
	Over, sideways and under on a magic carpet ride.
	A whole new world,
	A new fantastic point of view.
	No one to tell us no or where to go
	Or say we're only dreaming.
Jasmine:	A whole new world,
	A dazzling place I never knew.
	But when I'm way up here it's crystal clear
	That now I'm in a whole new world with you.
Aladdin:	Now I'm in a whole new world with you.
Jasmine:	Unbelievable sights, indescribable feeling.
	Soaring, tumbling, free-wheeling
	Through an endless diamond sky.
	A whole new world,
Aladdin:	Don't you dare close your eyes.
Jasmine:	A hundred thousand things to see.
Aladdin:	Hold your breath, it gets better.
Jasmine:	I'm like a shooting star I've come so far
	I can't go back to where I used to be.
Aladdin:	A whole new world.
Jasmine:	Every turn a surprise.
Aladdin:	With new horizons to pursue.
Jasmine:	Ev'ry moment red-letter.
Both:	I'll chase them anywhere. There's time to spare.
	Let me share this whole new world with you.
Aladdin:	A whole new world,
Jasmine:	A whole new world,
Aladdin:	That's where we'll be.
Jasmine:	That's where we'll be.
Aladdin:	A thrilling chase
Jasmine:	A wond'rous place
Both:	For you and me.

A Whale Of A Tale

From Walt Disney's
20,000 Leagues Under The Sea

Words and Music by AL HOFFMAN
and NORMAN GIMBEL

Got a whale of a tale to tell ya, lads, a whale of a tale or two ___ 'bout the flap-pin' fish and the girls I've loved, on nights like this with the moon a-bove, a whale of a tale and it's all true, I swear__ by my tat-too.

1. There was Mer - maid
2. There was Ty - phoon

Old Yeller
From Walt Disney's *Old Yeller*

Words by GIL GEORGE
Music by OLIVER WALLACE

Moderately bright

Old Yel - ler was a mon - grel, an ug - ly, lop - eared mon - grel;
Yel - ler was a hun - ter, a rar - in' tear - in' hun - ter; in

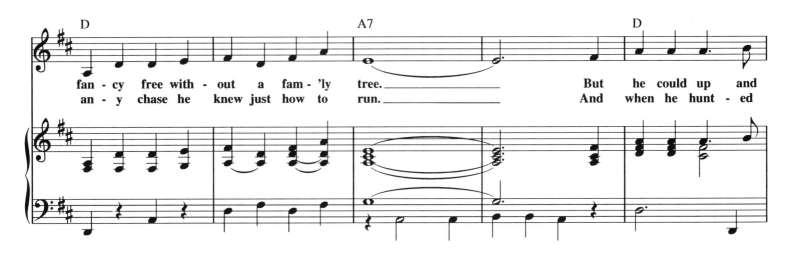

fan - cy free with - out a fam - 'ly tree. _____ But he could up and
an - y chase he knew just how to run. _____ And when he hunt - ed

do it and prove there's noth - ing to it, and that's how a good dog should
trou - ble he al - ways found it dou - ble, and that's when old Yel - ler had

Pretty Irish Girl

From Walt Disney's
Darby O'Gill And The Little People

Words by LAWRENCE E. WATKIN
Music by OLIVER WALLACE

Castle In Spain
From Walt Disney's *Babes In Toyland*

Words by MEL LEVEN
Music by GEORGE BRUNS
Adapted from a Victor Herbert Melody

Let's Get Together

From Walt Disney's *The Parent Trap*

Words and Music by RICHARD M. SHERMAN
and ROBERT B. SHERMAN

Moderate Rock tempo

Let's get to-geth-er. Yea, yea, yea! __
{ Why don't you and I com - }
{ Think of all that we could }

bine? __ }
share. _ }
Let's get to-geth-er.
{ What do you say? __ }
{ Ev -'ry day, __ }
We could have a swing-in'
ev -'ry way and ev -'ry -

time. __ We'd be a cra - a - a - zy team. Why don't we
where. _ And tho' we have - n't got a lot, we could be

Enjoy It!

From Walt Disney's
In Search Of The Castaways

Words and Music by RICHARD M. SHERMAN
and ROBERT B. SHERMAN

On The Front Porch

From Walt Disney's *Summer Magic*

Words and Music by RICHARD M. SHERMAN
and ROBERT B. SHERMAN

222

Fortuosity

From Walt Disney's *The Happiest Millionaire*

Words and Music by RICHARD M. SHERMAN
and ROBERT B. SHERMAN

Mickey Mouse March

From Walt Disney's *Mickey Mouse Club*

Words and Music by
JIMMIE DODD

The Ballad Of Davy Crockett

From Walt Disney's Television Series
Davy Crockett

Words by TOM BLACKBURN
Music by GEORGE BRUNS

Moderately

1. Born on a moun-tain top in Ten - nes - see, green - est state in the
2. eigh - teen - thir - teen the Creeks up - rose, addin' redskin arrows to the
3. Off through the woods _ he's a marchin' a - long, makin' up yarns an' a -
4. - 17. *(See additional lyrics)*

land of the free, raised in the woods so's he knew ev -'ry tree, kilt him a b'ar when
coun - try's _ woes. Now, In - jun fightin' is some - thin' he knows, so he should-ers his rifle an'
sing - in' a song, itch - in' fer fightin' an' right - in' a wrong, he's ringy as a b'ar an'

he was on - ly three. Da - vy, Da - vy Crock-ett, king of the wild fron -
off he _ goes. Da - vy, Da - vy Crock-ett, the man who _ don't know
twict as _ strong. Da - vy, Da - vy Crock-ett, the buck - skin _ buc - ca -

Additional Lyrics

4. Andy Jackson is our gen'ral's name,
   his reg'lar soldiers we'll put to shame.
   Them redskin varmints us Volunteers'll tame,
   'cause we got the guns with the sure-fire aim.
   Davy—Davy Crockett, the champion of us all!

5. Headed back to war from the ol' home place,
   but Red Stick was leadin' a merry chase,
   fightin' an' burnin' at a devil's pace
   south to the swamps on the Florida Trace.
   Davy—Davy Crockett, trackin' the redskins down!

6. Fought single-handed through the Injun War
   till the Creeks was whipped an' peace was in store.
   An' while he was handlin' this risky chore,
   made hisself a legend for evermore.
   Davy—Davy Crockett, king of the wild frontier!

7. He give his word an' he give his hand
   that his Injun friends could keep their land.
   An' the rest of his life he took the stand
   that justice was due every redskin band.
   Davy—Davy Crockett, holdin' his promise dear!

8. Home fer the winter with his family,
   happy as squirrels in the ol' gum tree,
   bein' the father he wanted to be,
   close to his boys as the pod an' the pea.
   Davy—Davy Crockett, holdin' his young 'uns dear!

9. But the ice went out an' the warm winds came
   an' the meltin' snow showed tracks of game.
   An' the flowers of Spring filled the woods with flame,
   an' all of a sudden life got too tame.
   Davy—Davy Crockett, headin' on West again!

10. Off through the woods we're ridin' along,
    makin' up yarns an' singin' a song.
    He's ringy as a b'ar an' twict as strong,
    an' knows he's right 'cause he ain' often wrong.
    Davy—Davy Crockett, the man who don't know fear!

11. Lookin' fer a place where the air smells clean,
    where the trees is tall an' the grass is green,
    where the fish is fat in an untouched stream,
    an' the teemin' woods is a hunter's dream.
    Davy—Davy Crockett, lookin' fer Paradise!

12. Now he's lost his love an' his grief was gall,
    in his heart he wanted to leave it all,
    an' lose himself in the forests tall,
    but he answered instead his country's call.
    Davy—Davy Crockett, beginnin' his campaign!

13. Needin' his help they didn't vote blind.
    They put in Davy 'cause he was their kind,
    sent up to Nashville the best they could find,
    a fightin' spirit an' a thinkin' mind.
    Davy—Davy Crockett, choice of the whole frontier!

14. The votes were counted an' he won hands down,
    so they sent him off to Washin'ton town
    with his best dress suit still his buckskins brown,
    a livin' legend of growin' renown.
    Davy—Davy Crockett, the Canebrake Congressman!

15. He went off to Congress an' served a spell,
    fixin' up the Gover'ments an' laws as well,
    took over Washin'ton so we heered tell
    an' patched up the crack in the Liberty Bell.
    Davy—Davy Crockett, seein' his duty clear!

16. Him an' his jokes travelled all through the land,
    an' his speeches made him friends to beat the band.
    His politickin' was their favorite brand
    an' everyone wanted to shake his hand.
    Davy—Davy Crockett, helpin' his legend grow!

17. He knew when he spoke he sounded the knell
    of his hopes for White House an' fame as well.
    But he spoke out strong so hist'ry books tell
    an' patched up the crack in the Liberty Bell.
    Davy—Davy Crockett, seein' his duty clear!

Theme From Zorro

From Walt Disney's Television Series *Zorro*

Guy Williams as Zorro;
from the colorized version of the
Walt Disney television series *Zorro*.

Words by NORMAN FOSTER
Music by GEORGE BRUNS

Out of the night when the full moon is bright

He is po - lite, but the wick - ed take

bright comes the

flight when they

horse - man know as Zor - ro.

catch the sight of Zor - ro.

DuckTales Theme

From Walt Disney's *The Disney Afternoon*

Words and Music by
MARK MUELLER

Bright rock

Life is like a hur-ri-cane_____ here in___ Duck-burg___
When it seems they're head-ing for_____ the fi-nal___ cur-tain,

race-cars, la-sers, aer-o-planes._____ It's a___ duck-blur___
cool de-duc-tion nev-er fails._____ That's for___ cer-tain___

might solve a mys-tery ___ or re-write his-tory.
the worst of mess-es ___ be-come suc-ces-ses.

Tale Spin Theme

From Walt Disney's *The Disney Afternoon*

Words and Music by MICHAEL SILVERSHER
and PATTY SILVERSHER

Golden Dream

From Walt Disney World's *Epcot Center*

Words by RANDY BRIGHT
Music by ROBERT MOLINE

It's A Small World

From The Disneyland And Walt Disney World
Attraction *It's A Small World*

Words and Music by RICHARD M. SHERMAN
and ROBERT B. SHERMAN

It's a world of laugh - ter, a world of
just one moon and one world gold - en

tears; it's a world of hopes and a world of fears. There's so
sun and a world smile means friend - ship to ev - 'ry - one, so though the

much that we share that it's time we're a - ware. It's a
moun - tains di - vide and the o - ceans are wide, it's a

Meet Me Down On Main Street

From Walt Disney's *Disneyland*

Words by TOM ADAIR
Music by OLIVER WALLACE

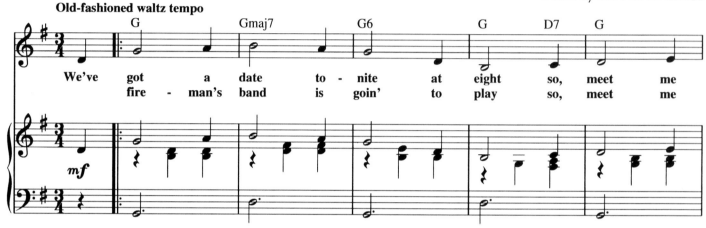

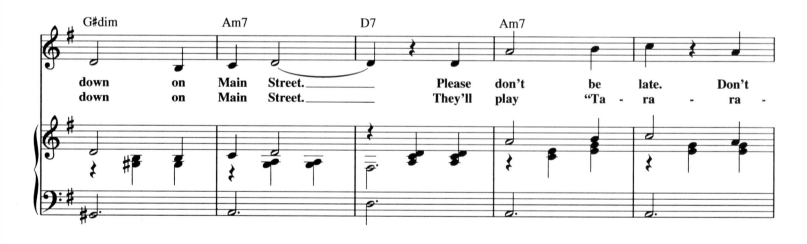

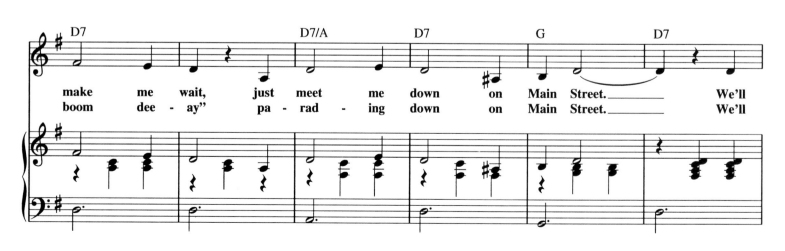

Old-fashioned waltz tempo

We've got a date to - nite at eight so, meet me
fire - man's band is goin' to play so, meet me

down on Main Street._____ Please don't be late. Don't
down on Main Street._____ They'll play "Ta - ra - ra -

make me wait, just meet me down on Main Street._____ We'll
boom dee - ay" pa - rad - ing down on Main Street._____ We'll

There's A Great Big Beautiful Tomorrow

From The Disneyland Attraction
Carousel Of Progress

Words and Music by RICHARD M. SHERMAN
and ROBERT B. SHERMAN

Brightly, with spirit

There's a great big beau-ti-ful to-mor-row ___ shin-ing at the end of ev-'ry day. ___ There's a great big beau-ti-ful to-mor-row ___ and to-mor-row's

8va lower

The Tiki Tiki Tiki Room

From The Disneyland And Walt Disney World Attraction
The Enchanted Tiki Room

Words and Music by RICHARD M. SHERMAN
and ROBERT B. SHERMAN

Yo Ho
(A Pirate's Life For Me)

From Walt Disney's
Disneyland and *Walt Disney World*

Words by XAVIER ATENCIO
Music by GEORGE BRUNS

SONG INDEX